Karen

**Other books by
Ann M. Martin**

P. S. Longer Letter Later
(written with Paula Danziger)
Leo the Magnificat
Rachel Parker, Kindergarten Show-off
Eleven Kids, One Summer
Ma and Pa Dracula
Yours Turly, Shirley
Ten Kids, No Pets
With You and Without You
Me and Katie (the Pest)
Stage Fright
Inside Out
Bummer Summer

For older readers:

Missing Since Monday
Just a Summer Romance
Slam Book

THE BABY-SITTERS CLUB series
THE BABY-SITTERS CLUB mysteries
THE KIDS IN MS. COLMAN'S CLASS series
BABY-SITTERS LITTLE SISTER series
(see inside book covers for a complete listing)

Little Sister

Karen's President
Ann M. Martin

Illustrations by Susan Crocca Tang

A
LITTLE APPLE
PAPERBACK

SCHOLASTIC INC.
New York Toronto London Auckland Sydney
Mexico City New Delhi Hong Kong

ISBN 0-590-50058-9

Copyright © 1998 by Ann M. Martin. Illustrations copyright © 1998 by Scholastic Inc. All rights reserved. Published by Scholastic Inc. THE BABY-SITTERS LITTLE SISTER, LITTLE APPLE PAPERBACKS, and associated logos are trademarks and/or registered trademarks of Scholastic Inc.

12 11 10 9 8 7 6 5 4 3 2 1   9/9 0 1 2 3/0

Printed in the U.S.A.   40
First Scholastic printing, February 1999

*The author gratefully acknowledges
Stephanie Calmenson
for her help
with this book.*

Switching Channels

I was cozy in my bed on a Saturday morning in February. My eyes were closed. I was dreaming that a fuzzy hat sat on my head. It felt nice and warm. I reached up to touch it. The hat nuzzled my hand and purred. Then it pounced onto my shoulder. I opened my eyes.

"You are not a fuzzy hat! You are Pumpkin!" I said. Pumpkin jumped off the bed and raced out of the room. It is hard to keep her in one place for very long. Pumpkin is a kitten — the cute black kitten who lives at

1

the big house. There are other pets here and some more at the little house. I will tell you about my houses and families and pets later. First I will tell you about me.

My name is Karen Brewer. I am seven years old. I have blonde hair, blue eyes, and a bunch of freckles. I am a glasses-wearer. I wear my blue glasses for reading. I wear my pink glasses the rest of the time. I do not need my glasses to sleep or to see the clock on my night table.

I turned to see what time it was. Hmm. It was almost eight o'clock. If I hurried down-stairs in my pajamas, I would be just in time to watch a rerun of *I Love Lucy*. That is one of my favorite TV shows.

I raced to the kitchen. Nannie was giving Emily Michelle her breakfast. (Nannie is my stepgrandmother. Emily is my little sis-ter.)

"Hi, Nannie! Hi, Emily!" I said. "I cannot eat breakfast with you. *I Love Lucy* is almost on!"

I filled a bowl with Krispy Krunchy cereal

and milk and headed for the den. I tried not to slosh milk on the way.

In the den, the TV was already on. Daddy and Elizabeth, my stepmother, were watching the news.

"Good morning, Karen," said Daddy. "How are you?"

"I am fine. But I wanted to watch *I Love Lucy*."

"Can you watch TV after the news?" asked Elizabeth. "It will be over in half an hour."

"But my show will be over then too," I said.

"Come sit and watch the news with us," said Daddy. "The weather is on now. But soon there will be a report about the President. He is visiting some countries in Europe over the weekend. It should be very interesting."

"I do not like the news so much," I replied. "Can I watch my show during the commercials?"

"That sounds fair," said Elizabeth.

I sat through the weather. It was going to be windy and cold. Then the newsman announced the upcoming story. It was about the President's arrival in France.

"We will be back with this story after the break," he said.

Daddy handed me the remote control. I switched to *I Love Lucy*. Lucy and her friend Ethel were stomping around barefoot in a barrel of grapes. They looked so funny. Their feet were purple up to their ankles! I watched for a couple of minutes. Then Daddy said, "I am sorry, Karen. It is time for us to switch back."

Boo. I wanted to see what Lucy was going to do next. But the next thing I knew, the President was on the screen, waving and smiling. His wife stood by his side. They looked very nice and friendly. But they were not funny. I wondered why Daddy and Elizabeth wanted to watch them instead of Lucy.

Soon another commercial came on. I switched to my station. But a commercial was on there too. I handed the remote back to Daddy.

"Thank you anyway," I said. "I think I will go get more cereal."

I went back to the kitchen and found the rest of my family there. I was glad. If I could not watch *I Love Lucy*, at least I could have fun with my brothers and sisters. I have a lot of them. Oh, right. I was going to tell you about my houses and families and pets. I will do that now.

The Karen Brewer Show

I Love Lucy is my favorite show because there is always something silly going on. There is usually something silly going on in my life too. That is what happens when you have two houses and two families.

A long time ago, things were quieter. I had one family and one house. The one family was Mommy, Daddy, Andrew, and me. (Andrew is my little brother. He is four going on five.) We lived here in this big house in Stoneybrook, Connecticut. It is the house Daddy grew up in.

Then Mommy and Daddy started arguing a lot. They tried to work things out, but they could not do it. They told Andrew and me that they loved us very much. But they did not want to be married to each other anymore. So they got divorced.

Mommy moved out with Andrew and me to a little house not far away. Soon she met a nice man named Seth. She and Seth got married, and now Seth is my stepfather.

That makes four people in the little house. We have some pets there too. They are Emily Junior, my rat; Bob, Andrew's hermit crab; Midgie, Seth's dog; and Rocky, Seth's cat. (Rocky is a lot older than Pumpkin, who is only a kitten.)

Daddy stayed in the big house after he and Mommy got divorced. Later he met and married Elizabeth, which is how she became my stepmother.

Elizabeth was married once before and has four children. They are my stepbrothers and stepsister. They are David Michael, who is seven like me; Kristy, who is thirteen and the best stepsister ever; and Sam and Charlie, who are so old they are in high school.

I already told you about Emily Michelle. She is two and a half. I love her so much that I named my rat after her. Daddy and Elizabeth adopted her from a faraway country called Vietnam.

Nannie, who is Elizabeth's mother, came to live at the big house to help with Emily Michelle. But really she helps with everyone.

Now I will tell you the names of the big-house pets. They are Shannon, David Michael's big Bernese mountain dog puppy; Scout, our training-to-be-a-guide-dog puppy; Crystal Light the Second, my goldfish; and Goldfishie, Andrew's flea. (Just kidding!)

Andrew and I switch houses almost every month. We spend one month at the big house, then one month at the little house. I gave us special names. I call us Andrew Two-Two and Karen Two-Two. (I thought up those names after my teacher read a book to our class. It was called *Jacob Two-Two Meets the Hooded Fang*.) I call us those names because we have two of so many things. We have two families, two mommies, and two daddies. We have two sets of toys and clothes and books. We have two bicycles, one at each house. I have two stuffed cats. Goosie lives at the little house. Moosie lives at the big house.

I also have two best friends. Hannie Papadakis lives across the street and one house over from the big house. Nancy Dawes lives next door to the little house. We spend so much time together that we call ourselves the Three Musketeers.

I was just finishing my second bowl of Krispy Krunchy cereal when I looked at Emily Michelle and burst out laughing. A banana was sticking out of her mouth and the peel was draped over her head. She was scratching her sides like a monkey.

I popped up from my chair and grabbed a banana from the fruit bowl. I copied Emily.

Sam passed out the rest of the bananas.

We all started jumping up and down, scratching our sides, and screeching. It sounded like a jungle.

"Help! I am living with a barrel of monkeys!" said Nannie.

Daddy and Elizabeth came to join the fun. We were definitely silly enough to be on TV. Who knows? Someday there could be a show about my family and me. Ladies and gentlemen, it is *The Karen Brewer Show!*

Saturday Plans

When the fun was over, everyone got dressed. Then I looked around for something fun to do. After all, it was Saturday.

Dingdong. The doorbell rang. I ran downstairs to see who was there. It was a couple of Sam's friends.

"Hi, Brian. Hi, Mark," I said.

"Hi, Karen. We came to help Sam with his campaign," said Brian.

"Here I am!" called Sam. "Come on up."

Sam had been talking all week long about

his campaign. The elections for his class officers were going to be held next month, and Sam wanted to be president. He and his friends were reading about winning campaigns to get ideas.

"Are you sure you do not want to hear about my class elections? There were some very excellent campaigns," I called up to Sam.

"Thank you. I am very sure," Sam replied.

I had asked Sam to listen to my ideas before. But he said he was not interested in ideas from second-graders. I told him he did not know what he was missing. But I did not really mind. Working on a campaign did not sound like Saturday fun to me.

I decided to see what Kristy was up to. If she did not have a baby-sitting job, maybe we could do something fun. (Kristy is the president of a sitting business she and her friends started. It is called the Baby-sitters Club.) Kristy's door was closed, so I headed for Andrew's room.

"What are you doing?" I asked.

"I am making rubbings of pennies," Andrew replied. He held up a penny. "Look. There is a President's head on it."

"I know," I said. "It is President Lincoln. We learned that at school."

Tracing Lincoln's head did not sound like Saturday fun to me either. I checked on David Michael. He was heading out with Charlie.

"Where are you two going?" I asked.

"We are going to the library," said Charlie. "I have to read about how a bill becomes a law."

"I thought a bill was what they give you when you eat at a restaurant," I replied.

"This is a different kind of bill," said Charlie.

"I am going to help with the assignment," said David Michael.

Just then Kristy came out of her room. She was dressed to go outside too.

"Are you going to baby-sit?" I asked.

"No. I am going to the library with Charlie and David Michael," Kristy replied. "I have to work on a school project about America's First Ladies."

"David Michael is helping Charlie. Can I help you?" I asked.

"Sure," replied Kristy. "Hurry and put your coat on. We have a lot to do."

My coat was on in no time. We said goodbye to Daddy and Elizabeth, then piled into the Junk Bucket. That is the name of Charlie's old car.

"What do you need to know about First Ladies?" I asked Kristy. "I can tell you who Jackie Kennedy was."

"I am sure you can. She was one of our most famous First Ladies. But there were others who did a lot to help our country," said Kristy. "Take Edith Gault Wilson, for example. She helped run the country when her husband was sick."

"Really? How did she know how to do that?" I asked.

"She worked closely with her husband

when he was well. So she knew a lot by the time he became sick," said Kristy.

A few minutes later we were pulling up in front of the library. We all had a lot of important work to do — even on Saturday!

Let's Go!

Saturday at the library turned out to be work *and* fun. My favorite parts were lunch and running into people we knew. That night at dinner, we all talked about our day.

"I still have not come up with a plan for my campaign," said Sam. "I have to do some more investigating."

"I learned about how a bill becomes a law," said Charlie.

"I had excellent pepperoni pizza!" I said.

When everyone finished laughing, Daddy

asked Charlie to tell us what he learned about bills becoming laws.

"It starts when someone has an idea he thinks should become a law. He contacts his local congressperson. If the congressperson likes the idea, he or she writes it up. Once the idea has been written up, it is called a bill. The bill is discussed in Congress. Congress is the House of Representatives and the Senate. The committees in Congress talk about the bill. If the bill gets a good report, the people in the House of Representatives vote on it. If they vote to pass the bill, it goes to the Senate. If the Senate votes to pass the bill, it goes to the President. The final decision is the President's. If the President signs the bill, it becomes a law."

"That was an excellent explanation," said Daddy. "As you will learn, the process becomes more involved as it goes along. But that is a very good start."

Next it was my turn to tell my family what I had learned. I told them a few things about First Ladies.

"Jacqueline Kennedy was called 'Number One Lady Goodwill Ambassador' because people in different countries liked her so much," I said. "And Eleanor Roosevelt wrote a book called *It's Up to the Women.* She said women are important to politics and the future of our country."

"That is excellent," said Elizabeth. "I notice that your projects all have something in common. They would all benefit from a trip to Washington, D.C."

"Did you say *trip*?" I shouted.

"Indoor voice, please, Karen," said Elizabeth. "The answer is yes, I did say trip. The question is when."

"School will be closed in a week for winter vacation," said Kristy.

"That is right. The first weekend of vacation is right before Presidents' Day," I said.

"That sounds like the perfect time for a visit to the capital," said Daddy. "Has anyone made other plans yet?"

No one had made any other plans.

"Then I suggest we take a vote," said

Daddy. "Whoever wants to go to Washington, D.C., say aye."

"Aye!" my whole family cried. (Except for Emily Michelle. She was napping in her high chair.)

"I will stay home for this trip," said Nannie. "I will watch Emily Michelle and the pets."

"Are you sure?" said Daddy. Nannie nodded. "The rest of us will go, then. Kids, Elizabeth and I will start planning our trip right away. We will let you know the details as soon as we have them."

That night Daddy and Elizabeth made lots of phone calls. On Sunday they told us the plan.

"We will leave early next Saturday. We will take the train from Stoneybrook to Grand Central Station in New York," said Daddy. "Then we will go to Penn Station and board the Amtrak train for Washington. The whole trip will take about five hours."

"I will call an old friend of mine who lives in Washington," said Elizabeth. "I am not sure what she is doing these days, but maybe she could show us around."

All right! I love taking trips. I could hardly wait to tell everyone at school about this.

Stumped

I decided I could not wait until Monday to tell Hannie and Nancy my great news. (We are all in Ms. Colman's second-grade class.) So instead of waiting, I called them each on Sunday night. Neither of them had plans yet for winter break. But they were both excited about mine. That is because they are my best friends.

The next morning I told a few of my classmates my news on the playground. I told Ms. Colman as soon as she walked into the room.

"That sounds wonderful, Karen," she

said. "I have an assignment to tell the class about later. You might be able to do some research on it while you are in Washington."

Cool! Now I would have important research to do, like my brothers and sister. But first I had an important assignment to do in class. It was my turn to take attendance. Ms. Colman handed me her book and a blue pencil. I started checking off names.

I checked my own name off first. Then I checked off the other kids who sit in the front row with me. (I used to sit at the back of the room with Hannie and Nancy. Then I got my glasses. Ms. Colman moved me up front where I could see better.)

I checked off Natalie Springer. I knew she was there, even though I could not see her face. She was ducking under her desk, pulling up her socks. Natalie's socks are always drooping.

I checked off Ricky Torres, my pretend husband. We got married on the playground one day at recess.

I checked off Addie Sidney. She was lining up pens and pencils on her wheelchair tray. She looked at me and smiled.

Next I checked off my best enemy. Her name is Pamela Harding. She can be a meanie-mo sometimes. Her friends are Jannie Gilbert and Leslie Morris. I checked off their names too.

I checked off Bobby Gianelli, Hank Reubens, and Omar Harris.

Terri and Tammy Barkan, who are twins, were in class. So was Audrey Green. Check. Check. Check.

I checked off Hannie and Nancy and waved to them.

I checked off a few more names before I handed the book and pencil back to Ms. Colman.

"Thank you, Karen," she said. "Now I would like to talk to you about your assignment for winter break. Presidents' Day is coming up, and I would like you to think about what you would do if you were elected President. Do any ideas come to mind?"

Omar Harris raised his hand.

"If I were President, I would make all school days into holidays. And I would make the holidays into school days," he said.

"That would not leave much time for school," said Ms. Colman.

"I know," said Omar, smiling. "School is fun, but holidays are the best!"

Ms. Colman called on Addie next.

"I would give all pets, including cats, dogs, birds, fish, and turtles, the right to vote," she said.

I thought this was an excellent idea. I knew Pumpkin would like it too. She would probably vote for tuna dinners every night. A few more kids had ideas. They were all good and funny.

"You are being very creative," said Ms. Colman. "But when you do the assignment, I would like you to be a little more serious."

Serious, creative . . . it did not matter to me. I usually have an idea a minute. But just then, I could not think of one single thing. I was stumped.

All Aboard!

I decided not to worry about my assignment yet. I was sure an idea would come to me while I was in Washington.

I crossed off the days on my calendar. Monday. Tuesday. Wednesday. Thursday. Friday.

On Friday night, Kristy came into my room to say good night.

"I am too excited to sleep," I said.

"But you will be too tired to have fun tomorrow if you stay up," Kristy replied. "I have an idea. Try counting train tickets."

Guess what. Kristy's idea worked! I told you she is the best stepsister ever. The next thing I knew, my alarm clock was ringing. It was Saturday morning. We were leaving for Washington, D.C., in just a few hours.

"Bring Emmie present," said Emily after breakfast.

"I will. I promise," I said.

I gave her a big hug. Then one for Nannie. And one for Pumpkin. One for Shannon. One for Scout.

"Karen, come on," said Daddy. "We do not want to miss our train."

"I will bring you a present too, Nannie!" I called as I raced out the door.

The trip to New York went fast. We reached Penn Station with time to spare. We kept our eyes on a big board that announced when trains were coming into and leaving the station. The board made a funny sound whenever the sign changed. *Thwunk. Thwunk, thwunk.* We all stood staring up at the sign. *Thwunk. Thwunk.*

"There is our train!" called Sam.

Train Number 103, bound for Washington, D.C., was on track number 8. Daddy boarded first and we followed him, looking for seats together.

"I want to sit by a window!" I called.

"There are four window seats, Karen," said Daddy. "You can slip in here."

I sat down and watched other people boarding the train. Then the conductor called, "All aboard for Washington, D.C.! All aboard!"

Soon the train started moving. It was so exciting!

"What should we do now?" I asked.

"I am going to do some schoolwork," said Kristy.

She took out her books and pulled down a tray to lean on. Sam and Charlie did the same thing. I could not believe it. They were no fun at all.

"I am hungry," said Andrew.

"Already?" asked Daddy. "The train just pulled out of the station."

"That is all right. I brought snacks," said

Elizabeth. She took juice and pretzels out of a bag. I had some too.

When I finished, I did not know what to do. Daddy and Elizabeth said I was not allowed to walk around the train. I thought about talking to the man and woman in front of me. But their noses were buried in their newspapers. So I drew pictures, played ticktacktoe with David Michael, read a book, went to the bathroom, and got a drink of water. Then I sat back and watched the cities go by. Trenton. Philadelphia. Zzzz. (No, that is not a city. I fell asleep.)

"Karen, wake up. We are almost there," said Kristy.

A couple of minutes later we pulled into Union Station in Washington, D.C. The station was the most beautiful I had ever seen. It was huge, with high ceilings and shiny marble floors. It felt like a museum, only it was full of restaurants and stores. It was just as beautiful outside, with big columns and carved eagles and statues.

"Look!" cried Andrew, pointing across the way. "The White House!"

"You are right that the building is white, Andrew," said Elizabeth. "But that building is called the Capitol. Congress meets there. And the President delivers his State of the Union address there."

This was a very important building, so I saluted it.

"I love Washington!" I said.

Company for Dinner

Daddy hailed two taxis for us and asked the drivers to take us to our hotel. It was in Georgetown, on M Street.

"Why are we leaving Washington?" asked David Michael.

"We are not leaving," Daddy replied. "Georgetown is the name of the Washington neighborhood we are staying in. It is old and pretty. And there is lots to do there."

"What does the M stand for?" I asked.

"I do not think it stands for anything," said Elizabeth. "It is just the name of the

33

street. I have seen most of the alphabet in Washington. But I do not remember seeing a B, J, X, Y, or Z Street."

"Someone did not know their letters," said Andrew.

He was singing the alphabet song as we pulled up to our hotel. The hotel looked very nice. But we did not stay there long. There was too much to do. We unpacked, ate a snack in the hotel restaurant, and went right back out.

"I made a dinner reservation at the other end of town," said Daddy. "We can work our way over there."

"Keep your eyes open for famous people," Kristy said.

I kept my eyes open for everything! I saw cute stores, street musicians, a flea market, and tons of restaurants.

"I would like to go to the Old Stone House," said Elizabeth. "It is the oldest building in the city. It was built before the American Revolution."

When we reached the building (it was on N Street), I felt as though I were in Massachusetts instead of Washington, D.C. The Old Stone House reminded me of a place there called Plimouth Plantation. I visited it once with Mommy, Seth, and Andrew. It is where the Pilgrims first landed in America.

The people at the Old Stone House were dressed in the same kind of old-fashioned clothes. They were cooking on an open fire, spinning, and quilting. I almost expected to see my Pilgrim friend, Remember. But I did not see her, and I did not see anyone famous.

When we left, we walked down a cobblestone street to Dumbarton Oaks, a huge mansion filled with paintings and old books. We looked around for awhile. Then we sat in the garden.

"I am hungry again," said Andrew.

"I made our reservation for an early dinner," said Daddy. "If we walk there, we will be right on time."

It was a long walk, but worth it. The Austin Grill was very cool. It was already crowded. I tugged on Kristy's sleeve.

"Do you see anyone famous yet?" I asked.

"Only in these pictures," she replied.

She pointed to a wall with photographs of singers and movie stars eating at the restaurant. There was even a picture of the Vice President.

We were taken to our table right away. I made sure to look at every person I passed. There was no one famous. (Daddy asked me not to stare while people were eating.)

The food was the Tex-Mex kind. I ordered corn soup, fried shrimp, and mashed potatoes. We all shared ice cream and double-dare chocolate cake for dessert. Yum.

"Does anyone need to use the bathroom before we go?" asked Elizabeth.

We took turns. I went upstairs with Kristy.

"This floor is roped off," she said. "I wonder why."

So did I. Maybe there was going to be a

birthday party. Or maybe someone famous was coming to dinner!

When we left, a crowd of people and three limousines were outside. I saw the back door of the restaurant slam shut.

"Who just went inside?" I asked a boy in the crowd.

"It was the President and his family," the boy replied.

"The President! Daddy, can we go back in?" I cried. "I think I forgot my sweater!" I said.

"You are wearing your sweater," said Elizabeth. "And no one is allowed to go in now."

Boo and bullfrogs. I *almost* saw the President. But almost does not count. I was going to have to keep trying.

Touring the City

When I opened my eyes the next morning, I did not see the big-house yard out my window. I saw the Potomac River!

"Hurry and get dressed, kids," said Daddy. "After breakfast we are going to the Mall."

"Who wants to go to a shopping mall in Washington, D.C.?" I said. "We can go to the mall anytime."

"This is not a shopping mall," replied Elizabeth. "The National Mall is a huge park. You will be amazed at what is there."

"At one end you can see the Capitol, which Andrew pointed out yesterday," said Daddy. "And there are museums on either side."

"There are monuments to four Presidents too," said Sam. "George Washington, Thomas Jefferson, Abraham Lincoln, and Franklin Roosevelt."

"And there is the Vietnam Veterans Memorial. And the Reflecting Pool," said Charlie.

"I am going to get dressed right now!" I said.

After breakfast, we headed for the Washington Monument. It is a shiny white marble tower in the sky.

"No building in Washington is allowed to be taller than the Washington Monument," said Daddy. "I read that it is five hundred and fifty-five feet high. There are eight hundred and ninety-seven steps to the top."

"I cannot climb that many steps! I did not eat enough breakfast," I said.

"We do not have to climb them. In fact,

we are not even allowed to," said Elizabeth. "There is an elevator."

That was a relief. We went inside the building and stood in line for the elevator. When it came, we zipped up. The elevator operator told us the ride took seventy seconds.

"It would have taken seventy *years* to climb to the top," I said.

When we stepped out of the elevator, we could see for miles and miles, every way we turned. We decided to look around on our own, instead of taking the tour.

"There is the Capitol again," said Daddy.

"That is my building!" said Andrew.

"Maybe you will work there someday," said Elizabeth.

"Nope. I want to be a fireman," replied Andrew.

Daddy pointed out part of the Smithsonian Institution. That is a group of museums. He showed us the Lincoln, the Jefferson, and the Vietnam Veterans memorials. Across the Potomac, in Virginia, we saw Arlington

National Cemetery, where Presidents and other famous people are buried.

"We can visit any of these places," said Daddy.

"I will skip the cemetery," I said. "I want to see famous people who are alive."

"Come look this way. There is the White House," said Daddy. "I will find out about visiting later in the week."

"Really? I did not think regular people could go in," I said.

"All you need is a ticket," said Daddy. "We will have to get in line early, but the visit will be worth it."

"Especially if I get to see the President," I added.

"I would not count on that, Karen," said Elizabeth. "The President is very busy running the country."

"He was not too busy to eat Tex-Mex food," I said. "Maybe if I write him a letter and tell him I will be there, he will come out and wave to me."

"The President gets hundreds of thousands of letters every day. He cannot possibly read and answer that many," said Sam.

Oh, well. Everyone was gigundoly excited about going to the White House. I was too. I would have fun even if I did not get to see the President.

9

Presidents, Presidents

After the Washington Monument, we went to the Vietnam Veterans Memorial. We saw statues of people who were in the Vietnam War. And we saw a special wall. Really it is two walls. They meet in a V. The walls are made of black stone and are covered with names. They are the names of the people who died in the war. The walls are very pretty and very sad. I took Elizabeth's hand.

"I want to look for Hannie's uncle George," I said. "Her father told us he died in that war."

44

I could not find his name on the wall. But Elizabeth helped me find it in a special book. The book told us where it was on the wall.

We did not talk much. We just looked.

We went to the Lincoln Memorial next. It looked very important. Lots of white columns were holding up the roof. I knew I had seen the building before. Suddenly I remembered where. I asked Daddy for a penny.

"Look, Andrew. This building is on the back of the penny."

"I read that the columns stand for the states that existed when Lincoln died," said Charlie. "There were thirty-six states then."

"There are fifty states now," I said.

"I knew that," said David Michael.

Inside the building, we saw a statue of President Lincoln sitting in a big armchair.

"President Lincoln did many good things for our country," said Elizabeth. "One of the most important things he did was to help end slavery. People were very sad when

Abraham Lincoln was killed by a gunshot."

"My teacher likes to tell our class some-thing Lincoln once said," said Charlie. "He said 'Work, work, work, is the main thing.' "

Hmm. That reminded me of Ms. Colman. And my assignment. I still had to think of what I would do if I were President. If I thought of something very good, maybe someone would make a statue of me!

I did not have time to think much then. We were on our way to more memorials.

We stopped and had a picnic lunch on the Mall. Then we went to the Roosevelt Memo-rial and the Jefferson Memorial. I learned a lot of interesting things about our Presi-dents.

I learned that Franklin Delano Roosevelt caught a disease called polio and could hardly walk without leg braces or a wheel-chair. But that did not stop him from becom-ing President. He was an excellent President too.

I learned that Thomas Jefferson wrote the Declaration of Independence.

"He was a fine speaker and writer," said Daddy. "He said many things way back in the 1800s that we still say now. Let me see if I can remember something. Oh, yes. Thomas Jefferson said, 'Delay is preferable to error.'"

Maybe Thomas Jefferson had been talking about homework assignments. He would have wanted me to think carefully about my project instead of rushing into anything by mistake. Still, I would have to come up with an idea sometime.

Elizabeth's Friend

I thought a little about my assignment, but not a lot. I was just too busy. (I wonder what Thomas Jefferson would have said about that.)

Back at the hotel, we found a message for Elizabeth. Her friend, Marsha Meyers, wanted to meet us for dinner.

"That will be wonderful," said Elizabeth, when she called back. "We can eat right downstairs."

We showered, dressed, and waited in the dining room for Marsha to arrive. When she walked into the room, Elizabeth jumped up and ran to her. They hugged and started talking and giggling. Elizabeth had told us they had not seen each other for a long time. I would probably act the same way if I had not seen Hannie or Nancy for a long time. (I promised myself I would try never to let that happen.) Elizabeth introduced us to Marsha.

"Marsha and I had a chance to catch up a little on the phone this afternoon. It turns out that Marsha is a researcher at the White House," said Elizabeth.

"Do you ever get to see the President?" I asked.

"Yes, I do. He consults with me fairly often when he needs information about projects he is working on," replied Marsha.

"That is so cool!" I said. "Could you introduce me to him? I have a lot of questions to ask him."

"I would love to introduce you, Karen. But I cannot bring guests to my work meetings," said Marsha.

"What kind of information does the President need for his projects?" asked Charlie.

"Well, for his last trip to Europe, he asked me to find out about the countries he would be visiting and the officials he would be meeting," said Marsha.

"What is the President like?" asked Kristy.

"He is a considerate person and very smart," said Marsha. "He wants the best for the American people."

"Does he have any pets?" asked Andrew.

"He and the First Lady and their daughter have a very cute beagle puppy named Oscar," said Marsha. "And his daughter, who is nine, has her own turtle, named Boxer."

"Does he have hobbies?" asked David Michael.

"The President plays chess, reads all kinds of books, and likes to listen to all kinds of music," said Marsha.

"Does he ever watch TV? Does he have a favorite show?" I asked.

"Yes, he watches TV. He watches the news

and he likes some sitcoms," said Marsha. "I know he enjoys reruns of *I Love Lucy*."

"The President watches the same show I watch!" I said.

"The President is a very good speaker," said Daddy. "Do you help him with the research for his speeches?"

"Yes, that is a large part of my job," said Marsha. "You might be interested to know that while he looks calm on TV, he really gets very nervous before he makes a speech."

We asked lots more questions. I loved hearing about the President. He was a real person. I used to think that teachers were not real people. Then I got to know Ms. Colman and her family. I found out that teachers are real people. Now I was finding out the same thing about Presidents.

"Um, do you think you will be speaking to the President while we are here in Washington?" I asked. "If you do, could you ask if you could bring one guest?"

"Karen, Marsha already said she could not do that," said Daddy.

"I can try to arrange for you all to have a private tour of the White House, though," said Marsha. "That way you will not have to stand in line with thousands of other people, waiting for tickets."

"That would be wonderful! Thank you," said Elizabeth.

When dinner was over, Marsha promised to call soon to make plans. Even though I was not going to meet the President, a private White House tour would be pretty exciting. And maybe the President would be there that day. Maybe I would see him.

Karen's Ideas

On Monday, Elizabeth, Sam, Charlie, and Kristy went to the National Museum of American History.

Daddy took Andrew, David Michael, and me to the National Air and Space Museum. It was a very cool place. It also looked like a good place to find ideas for my school project. I needed to think about what I would do if I were President.

The first thing we did at the museum was touch a four-billion-year-old moon rock.

"Is this really and truly from the moon?" I asked.

"Yes, it is," replied Daddy.

"How many birthdays is four billion?" asked Andrew.

"A lot," said Daddy.

He led us to the *Skylab* exhibit next. *Skylab* was a space station that orbited Earth in the 1970s. We got to see what it was like to live in space.

"Karen Brewer calling ground control. Ground control, do you read me?" I said in my official astronaut voice.

"Reading you loud and clear," replied David Michael. "Please bring back a large supply of moon pies for dessert."

"Moon pies coming right up!" I said.

Space travel was fun. And educational. Maybe if I were President, I could send every American citizen to the moon. No. That would cost a lot of money. Anyway, most people are too busy for a long trip. I needed another idea.

Next we saw the Wright brothers' airplane. It is called the *Flyer.* In 1903 it became the first plane to fly under its own power. Then we saw Amelia Earhart's plane. She flew all by herself across the Atlantic Ocean. That was very brave.

Inside a huge theater, we saw a movie about flight.

Then, in honor of the Wright brothers, we had lunch at a very nice restaurant called Wright Place.

I liked the Air and Space Museum a lot. But I left without an idea for my assignment.

"Next stop, Museum of Natural History," said Daddy.

Andrew became excited as soon as we entered the building.

"Look at that elephant!" he said.

"This is just like the museum in New York," said David Michael.

"It is very much like the one in New York," said Daddy. "But each museum has things that are special. One of the most special exhibits here is in the Gems and Minerals room. Come, I will show you."

Daddy showed us the world's largest crystal ball. (In a book I had just read called *The Gator Girls*, two friends visit a fortune-teller named Madame Lulu. If Madame Lulu had had a crystal ball that big, she could have seen lots of things.)

I wished the crystal ball had the answer to my school-assignment problem. I gazed into it, but I did not see any messages.

"Karen, we are over here," called Daddy.

He was standing in front of a case with a huge diamond inside it.

"Kids, this is the Hope Diamond. It is the largest blue diamond in the world," said Daddy.

"It is beautiful," I said. "But I do not think such a big diamond would be very comfortable to wear."

"You are right. It is also supposed to bring bad luck to the wearer," said Daddy.

I stepped back. I do not like things that

bring bad luck. Who would? That gave me an idea. If I were President, I could order the Hope Diamond to be moved out of Washington, D.C. That would keep me, the President of the United States, safe. That would be important to the country and the world.

I was about to tell my idea to Daddy when I thought of something. If I moved the diamond someplace else, the people who lived in that place would be mad at me. Also I did not think Ms. Colman would like the idea. Moving a diamond did not seem like a very good use of my presidential powers.

Boo. I had wasted five minutes thinking about the diamond. That was bad luck, and I was not even wearing the diamond.

Sam I Am!

Guess who we ran into when we left the Natural History Museum? Sam and Charlie. After they had finished visiting the National Museum of American History with Elizabeth and Kristy, they had gone exploring on their own.

"We were going to sit down somewhere for hot chocolate," said Daddy. "Would you like to join us?"

"Sure," said Charlie. "Thanks."

It was a cold and damp Washington day.

Hot chocolate was just what we needed. We sat in a coffee-and-bookshop. It was very cozy.

"We saw some great things at the National Museum of American History," said Sam. "I even came up with a few ideas for my campaign."

"I did not have any ideas for my school assignment," I said.

"Maybe you should go to the National Museum of American History tomorrow. You might be inspired," said Charlie.

"Look at the button I bought," said Sam. "It is a copy of one from Dwight Eisenhower's presidential campaign."

He held up a red, white, and blue button that said, I LIKE IKE.

"Ike is the nickname Dwight Eisenhower was given when he was a boy. It made a very catchy campaign slogan," said Charlie.

"I need a catchy slogan too," said Sam.

"I have an idea!" I said. "Your slogan could be *Sam I Am!*"

It was a lot easier helping with someone

else's assignment than it was doing my own.

"That is not bad," said Sam. "I will think about it."

"If you do not like that one, you could try *Bam! Vote for Sam!* Or, *In a Jam? Vote for Sam!*" I said.

"I think I like *Sam I Am!* best. Thank you, Karen," said Sam.

"You are welcome," I replied.

"Where else did you go today?" asked Daddy.

"We went into the Capitol," replied Charlie. "It is an amazing place. It is the second-oldest building in Washington."

While he was there Charlie learned about some bills that had been passed recently. Sam told us about the progress he was making on his assignment. Andrew had traced the Lincoln Memorial from a penny for show-and-tell. And David Michael was going to make a space-walk diorama to share with his class.

That left me. I still did not know what I

would do if I were President. If I could not think of something, maybe I would be impeached. (That is when someone important in government is fired. I learned that from Sam at dinner the night before.) I did not want to be impeached. It sounded very embarrassing.

The President's Schedule

The six of us went back to the hotel after our hot-chocolate break. Elizabeth and Kristy were already there.

"You will not believe who we just missed seeing again!" said Kristy.

"You mean you almost saw the President?" I asked.

"Yup. We heard that he led a group of schoolchildren through the Library of Congress just before we arrived."

"I wish I could have been there!" I said.

"Do not feel too bad," said Elizabeth.

"You are going to do something exciting the day after tomorrow. Marsha has set up our private tour for Wednesday afternoon."

"Really? Will the President be there that day?" I asked. "I know I cannot meet with him. But maybe I could just *see* him."

"Marsha did not say she was meeting with the President on Wednesday. I am not sure if he will be around," said Elizabeth.

"Can you call her and ask her? Please?" I said.

"I am sorry, Karen. I do not want to bother Marsha. It is very nice of her to go to the trouble of setting up this special tour," said Elizabeth. "We should not ask her for anything more."

"I have an idea," said Daddy. "If we look in the newspaper, we might be able to find out about the President's schedule. It might say something about his being at the White House on Wednesday."

"Can we go buy the newspaper now?" I asked.

"We should get ready for dinner now.

On the way out, we can stop at the news-stand and pick up a copy of the paper," said Daddy.

"But the newsstand may be all out of newspapers by then. It may even be closed," I said.

"If it is okay with you, I will take Karen down for the paper now," Kristy said to Daddy. "We cannot all shower at the same time anyway."

"Okay," said Elizabeth. "That is a good idea."

Kristy and I hurried down to the hotel newsstand. On the way, we passed the gift shop. I noticed some excellent gifts in the window. I saw a Washington, D.C., place mat that would be perfect for Emily Michelle. (She could spill her chocolate milk on lots of important places.) There was a navy blue drinking mug for Nannie with a picture of the White House on it. And there was a gigundoly gorgeous American flag hair barrette. That would be perfect for Hannie, Nancy, and me. I had brought some money with me to Washington. If the gifts were not too expensive, I could buy them all.

When we found the newsstand, I saw that we were in luck. It was open and the paper was there.

"I hope there is something in it about the President's schedule," said Kristy.

She bought a copy of *The Washington Post*. We took it upstairs and handed it to Daddy. We thought he could find what we needed faster than we could.

Daddy turned one page after another. He did not say a word. Then he stopped turning and started reading.

"Here it is," he said. "There is an article about the President's schedule. He will be meeting with the Vice President and Secretary of State at the White House on Wednesday afternoon."

I was so excited I could hardly stand it!

"What time are we going to be there?" I asked.

"Our tour is scheduled for three o'clock," said Elizabeth.

"Yippee! The President will be at the White House," I said. "And I will be there too."

Oh, Say Can You See!

I decided Tuesday was definitely the day I would have an idea for my school assignment. After all, we were going to the National Museum of American History. That is where Sam got ideas for his campaign.

Before we left, I put a pad and pencil in my backpack. That way I could write down my ideas and not forget them.

But as soon as we reached the museum, my assignment flew out of my brain. There was too much else to think about.

"We have arrived at just the right time,"

said Kristy. (She had come back to the museum with us to do more research on the First Ladies.) "If we hurry, we can see the flag! They show it every hour, and it is just ten o'clock now."

She led us to a place where a curtain was being opened. Behind the curtain was a gigantic flag with stars and stripes. It looked like the flag at school, but there were not as many stars.

"That is the very flag that inspired Francis Scott Key to write our national anthem, 'The Star-Spangled Banner,' " said Daddy. "It had fifteen stars for fifteen states."

The flag did not stay out very long.

"Why are they hiding it?" asked Andrew.

"They are not hiding it. They are protecting it," said Kristy. "It is very old and not too strong."

"That was neat," said David Michael. "What is next?"

"Follow me," said Kristy.

I was glad my big sister had been to the museum the day before. She knew all the best things to see. This time she took us to a big gold ball that was swinging back and forth.

"This is a Foucault pendulum," said Daddy. "It is a copy of a pendulum that was on view in France in the 1800s."

"What is a pendala?" asked Andrew.

"A pendulum is an object that swings back and forth while the earth turns beneath it," said Daddy.

Andrew looked confused. I was a little confused too. But I still liked watching the pendulum. Back and forth. Back and forth. I started swaying with it. Then I had to shake myself awake so I would not be hypnotized.

"I would like to go to the First Ladies exhibit now," said Kristy. "Will you come with me?"

We were happy to go. On the way we saw the ruby slippers Dorothy wore in *The Wizard of Oz.*

"They look just my size!" I said.

Andrew was excited to see Mister Rogers's sweater.

Finally we made it to the First Ladies exhibit. Kristy took out her pad and pencil and started writing notes.

We saw the gowns the First Ladies wore to important events. They were gigundoly beautiful. And we read about important things First Ladies have done.

Mrs. Eisenhower liked children. She brought the Easter Egg Roll back to the White House. (It had been stopped because of a war.) Mrs. Nixon encouraged people to volunteer to help others. And Mrs. Reagan led a campaign for kids and grown-ups to "just say no" to drugs.

First Ladies did a lot of good things. But it was not time to think about being a First Lady. I had to think about being President. What I would do? I still did not know.

Read All About It

We had planned to meet back at the hotel for lunch.

"Daddy, will you buy the newspaper again today?" I asked. "I want to be sure the President's schedule has not changed."

"Sure. I would like to read the paper anyway," replied Daddy.

He stopped at the newsstand in the hotel. We sat and read the newspaper in the lobby while we waited for Elizabeth, Sam, and Charlie to return.

"There is good news on page five," said

Daddy. "The President is still scheduled to have his meeting at the White House tomorrow afternoon."

"Excellent!" I said. "Now all we have to do is be in the exact right place at the exact right time."

"Do not get your hopes too high," said Daddy. "It is not likely that you will get to see the President, even if he is there. The White House is a big place, and there are lots of closed doors."

"Can we open them?" I asked.

"Absolutely not! We must remember that we are guests," said Daddy. "Now, would you like to read about the meeting yourself?"

"Okay," I replied.

I took the newspaper and read all about the President's meeting. He was going to talk with the Vice President and the Secretary of State about some faraway countries that were having trouble getting along. The President was going to try to help them make peace. That sounded like a very good thing for a President to do.

I turned the page to read some more. I could hardly believe it. I had learned so much in Washington that now I liked reading the news. I felt very grown-up reading *The Washington Post* in the lobby of a fancy hotel.

The next article I read was about Presidents' Day and how people were going to observe it. The President and the First Lady were going to Arlington Cemetery. (I remembered seeing the cemetery from the Washington Monument.) Then the First Lady was going to visit a children's hospital. She was going to read to the children at the hospital library.

"First Ladies do a lot of nice things," I said.

The minute I said it, I knew that was it! I had the idea I needed for my assignment. And I loved it!

Just then Elizabeth, Sam, and Charlie showed up.

"Listen to my idea!" I said. "If I were President, I would declare a holiday in honor of First Ladies. That is because they do so many good things."

"That sounds terrific," said Elizabeth.

"No, wait! I have an even better idea. I would declare a holiday for Presidents' Partners," I said. "Then if I were President and had a husband, it would be his holiday too."

"Bravo, Karen Brewer!" said Daddy.

I stood up and took a bow. Then I sat down in my chair again. What a relief. It was Tuesday, and I had the idea for my assignment, just like I had planned.

At the Zoo

On Wednesday morning we went to the National Zoo. We decided to stay together because it was the day of our visit to the White House.

I love animals. But I was too excited to have a very good visit.

"Hello, Hsing-Hsing!" I called. "I am going to the White House this afternoon!"

Hsing-Hsing did not look too interested in my news. That is because it was his feeding time. Hsing-Hsing is a giant panda who was a gift from China. He eats bamboo. A sign said that he eats thirty pounds of bamboo a day. *Chomp, chomp, chomp.* Pandas are very cute. And this one was very hungry.

Next we saw some elephants. I told them my news.

"I am going to the White House this afternoon!" I said.

Two of the elephants trumpeted. I think they were telling me to have a good time.

"Thank you!" I replied.

We saw kangaroos, camels, antelopes, hippos, rhinos, giraffes. It was a sunny day and the animals were out in open spaces. It was the perfect day for a visit to the zoo. I tried my best to concentrate.

Roar! That got my attention.

A group of lions was out grazing. I watched the one lion who was doing all the roaring. I could tell he was in charge. He was probably the president lion.

"Can we go back to the hotel soon? We need to get ready," I said.

"Karen, it is eleven-thirty. We are not due

at the White House until three," said Daddy.

"But I need time to get dressed. I want to look nice when I see the President," I said.

"We promise to leave enough time for you to get ready," said Elizabeth. "But it would be silly to go back now and waste such a beautiful morning indoors."

Right after Elizabeth said that, we headed inside the bat cave. It was very dark. But we did not stay long because Andrew was scared.

Our next stop was at the wetlands exhibit. We saw beautiful birds there. We watched a brown pelican flying above the water.

"He is going after his meal," said Sam.

The pelican looked at the water, then swooped down.

"He sees his lunch!" said Charlie.

The pelican dipped down and came up with a fish. It disappeared down his long bill.

"I think it is time for our lunch too," said

Elizabeth. "If we eat now, Karen, there will be plenty of time for you to get ready."

"Good-bye, National Zoo!" I said. "I am sorry it was such a short visit. But I have places to go and an Important Person to meet!"

The White House Tour

At 1:35 on Wednesday afternoon I was putting my new American flag barrette into my hair. Daddy had let me stop at the hotel gift shop to buy it. It was just what I needed to complete my red, white, and blue White House Visiting Day outfit.

"You look wonderful, Karen," said Kristy.

"Thank you. You do too," I replied.

It was 1:42 when we left our hotel room. I pushed the elevator button about six times in a row.

"Easy, Karen. We have plenty of time," said Daddy.

"There could be traffic on the way," I replied. "There is already traffic in the elevator. It is taking forever."

The elevator came a minute later. We got taxis right away. I was in a taxi with Daddy, Andrew, and Kristy.

"We would like to go to the White House, please," said Daddy.

I wished he had let me say that! It sounded gigundoly important.

We drove a few city blocks, then turned onto a bigger road. *Honk!* Drivers all around were blowing their horns.

"There may have been an accident up ahead," said the taxi driver. "We will have to be patient."

"We do not have time!" I said.

"I am afraid we have no choice," said the driver.

He inched along. Finally the traffic jam cleared. We pulled up to the White House at 2:15.

I had never visited a house like this before. Usually I just walk into a house and say hello. Here we had to be checked for dangerous or messy things. For example, we were not allowed to have chewing gum or food. That was okay, because we had already eaten our lunch. We were not allowed to bring big knives or guns or firecrackers. That was okay too, because we are never allowed to have those things. And I did not want them.

Marsha was waiting for us at the end of the security checks. She was standing with a young man.

"Welcome," she said. "I would like you to meet your tour guide."

"Just follow me," he said. "I will be happy to answer any questions you have."

"Have you seen the President yet today?" I asked.

"Karen, we are touring the White House. We are not looking for the President," said Daddy.

Boo. I knew I could not ask any more

questions about finding the President. But I could still look.

Our tour guide told us about the First Families who have lived in the White House. And he showed us some things the First Ladies had done to make the White House look nice.

"When Mrs. Eisenhower lived here, she used pink so much that people called the color 'Mamie pink.' Mamie was her nickname. She was so careful about keeping the house looking nice that people had to walk around the edges of rooms to keep from leaving footprints on the carpet."

"She would not have been very happy at our house. We have people and pets running all over the place," I said.

We visited a few rooms. We went to the Green Room, Blue Room, Red Room, State Dining Room, and East Room.

"Um, how many rooms are there?" I asked.

I did not say anything about seeing the

President. But I thought if we visited every room, we could find him.

"There are one hundred and thirty-two rooms at the White House," said the guide. "We are allowed in only a few of them."

I was disappointed. The tour was fun. But I had wanted to see the President. After all, I knew from reading the newspaper that he was right in the building.

We were on our way to the gift shop when we heard someone calling Elizabeth. It was Marsha.

"I am so glad I found you," she said. "Come with me. There is someone I would like you to meet."

Greetings, Mr. President

Marsha led us to a room we had not been in before. Sitting in an armchair with his back to us was a man looking at some papers.

"Excuse me, Mr. President. Your visitors are here," said Marsha.

Mr. President! I could not believe it. The man stood up and turned around. It was him. It was the real, live President of the United States! He smiled at us.

"Welcome to the White House," he said.

"I am happy to meet special friends of Ms. Meyers."

"We are happy to meet you too!" I said.

No one else in my family said anything. For a minute they were speechless. Then the President shook hands with each of us.

"This is a great honor, Mr. President," said Daddy.

"Thank you for seeing us," said Elizabeth.

"I rarely have a chance to meet with visitors to the White House," said the President. "I am glad I could make the time today. I understand there is someone here who has a lot of questions for me. I will be happy to answer any questions I can."

The President turned and looked at me.

"Thank you!" I said. "My first question is, do you like being President of the United States? I want to know in case I want to be President someday. And, um, could you please answer slowly? I want to write everything down."

I took out my notepad and pencil.

"Karen, I am glad you are thinking about

becoming President. I like my job very much," the President replied. "And I notice that you are very good at speaking up. That is an important skill for a President to have."

"Sometimes I get in trouble for speaking up too much," I replied.

"Me too," said the President.

He laughed. I could see we had a lot in common.

"Karen, maybe someone else has something to say," said Daddy.

The rest of my family asked their questions. A couple of times I asked the President if he could please slow down so I could take notes. He was very patient.

Then it was my turn again. I told the President about Ms. Colman and our homework assignment.

"What do you think of my idea to have a Presidents' Partners' Day?" I asked.

"I think you have an excellent idea, Karen," replied the President. "If that proposal came to me as a bill from Congress, I would sign it right away."

Wow! If my idea was good enough to be signed by the President, I was sure it was good enough to share with my class at school.

"It has been a great pleasure speaking with you," said the President. "I wish I could talk with you longer. But I have a meeting scheduled with the Vice President and the Secretary of State."

"We read all about your meeting," I said. "You are going to talk about countries that are not getting along."

"I see you keep up with the news. We need more citizens like you. Thank you, Karen," said the President.

"You are welcome!" I replied.

Visitors are not usually allowed to take photographs at the White House. But the President made an exception to the rule, since we are Marsha's friends. Daddy took a picture of the President shaking my hand. *Snap!*

Getting Ready

We thanked Marsha and headed back to our hotel. We had an early supper, then went to bed. It had been a long day, and we were going to catch a train back to New York first thing in the morning.

I spent part of my time on the train reading over my notes. The rest of the time I looked out the window, remembering my visit with the President of the United States.

"Nannie, guess what!" I called as soon as we got home. "We met the President!"

"That is wonderful!" Nannie replied. "Come tell us all about it."

I gave Nannie and Emily their gifts. (They loved them.) While we ate lunch, we all told them about our visit to Washington.

I called Hannie and Nancy after lunch and told them my news too. Then I got to work. My presentation was due on Monday.

I started writing about my idea for a new national holiday. I read what I wrote aloud to see how it sounded. It sounded very good. But it needed something more.

Hearing the President tell me he liked my idea had been so exciting. Reading it on paper was just not the same. I wished I had taken a tape recorder to the White House. Then I could play the tape for my class.

"Wait a minute! I have an idea," I said.

I ran downstairs to find Daddy. He was part of my idea. Daddy was in his office catching up on some paperwork.

"Daddy, could you please help me with my assignment?" I asked.

"I would be happy to," replied Daddy. "What would you like me to do?"

"I would like you to play the part of the President on a tape I am going to make for my class," I said. "I have notes from our real meeting, and I can write a script for you."

"That sounds like a lot of fun," said Daddy. "Just let me know when you are ready."

"Thank you!" I said.

I was having fun doing my assignment. I made up a very neat script. I wrote the name of the person who was speaking. Then I wrote down the exact words that were said.

When the script was ready, I went back to Daddy's office. We closed the door and got to work making my tape.

Soon I was finished. I had my written report and my tape recording. And our photos would be ready on Saturday.

Presidents' Partners' Day

We did not give our reports right away on Monday. Ms. Colman said we were still too excited from our vacations.

"I think you need some time to settle down," she said.

I had trouble settling down in the afternoon too. So Ms. Colman did not call on me first. That was okay. I liked listening to the other reports. And if I went last, my report would be an excellent surprise.

"Omar, would you like to begin?" asked Ms. Colman.

Omar walked to the front of the room and read his report.

"If I were President, I would make tax cuts," he said.

He went on to describe how upset his parents get at tax time. This upsets his whole family, including their pets.

"So it would be a very good thing for everyone to cut taxes. And that is what I would do if I were President. Thank you," said Omar.

"That was a good report," said Ms. Colman. "It raises some interesting questions about our country's policy on taxes. Some people think we need to leave taxes as they are, to pay for services in our country. Other people think taxes are just too high. Addie, would you like to speak next?"

Addie spoke about animal rights.

"If I were President, I would make sure I represented animals as well as people," she said. "We should consider animals citizens too."

Nancy spoke about gun control.

"If I were President, I would make it very hard for people to get guns, because they hurt and kill people," she said.

"Thank you, Nancy," said Ms. Colman. "That is another interesting issue. Some people think everyone should be allowed to own a gun for protection. Other people, like you and me, think guns are too dangerous to have in the hands of so many people."

I liked every one of the reports I heard. Finally it was time for me to give mine.

"I will tell you what I would do if I were President. Then I will let you hear the President's own words," I said. "The voice you will be hearing is my daddy's. But the words are the President's, because I got to meet him last week and I wrote down everything he said."

"Is that true, Karen? You met the President?" asked Ms. Colman.

"Yes, I did!" I replied.

Nancy and Hannie had done a very good job of keeping my secret. Everyone, including Ms. Colman, was surprised and excited.

"Please go ahead with your report," said Ms. Colman. "We are looking forward to hearing your idea."

"If I were President, I would declare a new holiday. It would be Presidents' Partners' Day, because of all the good things Presidents' partners have done."

I played my tape for the class. They heard Daddy's voice speaking the President's words.

"I think you have an excellent idea, Karen. If that proposal came to me as a bill from Congress, I would sign it right away."

While they listened, I held up the photograph of the President shaking my hand. It was almost as though he were in the room with us.

The class clapped when my report was through.

"Thank you, Karen," said Ms. Colman. "If you ever become President, or the President's partner, our country will be very lucky."

Ms. Colman said she liked many of our ideas.

"Maybe someday your ideas will become bills that are turned into laws," said Ms. Colman.

Wow! I had met the President. I had presented a good report. I was a very proud citizen.

L. GODWIN

About the Author

ANN M. MARTIN lives in New York City and loves animals, especially cats. She has two cats of her own, Gussie and Woody.

Other books by Ann M. Martin that you might enjoy are *Stage Fright*; *Me and Katie (the Pest)*; and the books in *The Baby-sitters Club* series.

Ann likes ice cream and *I Love Lucy*. And she has her own little sister, whose name is Jane.

Little Sister

Don't miss #107

KAREN'S COPYCAT

I started shaping my clay the way Merry had. I formed the beginnings of a round body, four short flippers, a head, and a stumpy tail.

After a few minutes, Andrew leaned over and whispered, "Psst! Karen! What are you making?"

"A sea turtle," I whispered back.

"Oh," he said.

I looked at Andrew's clay. It was a big lump with pointy ears and holes for eyes.

"What are you making?" I asked. "A really fat cat or dog?"

"No," he said, mushing his clay back into a ball. "I am making a sea turtle too."

He had not been making a sea turtle until I told him I was making one. He was copying again!

Little Sister

by Ann M. Martin
author of The Baby-sitters Club®

More Titles... ➡